A Safe Place

Maxine Trottier

illustrated by Judith Friedman

Albert Whitman & Company,

Morton Grove, Illinois

To learn the name and telephone number of a U. S.
women's shelter near you, call the National Domestic
Violence Hotline at 1-800-799-7233. In Canada,
call your local emergency services number.

Library of Congress Cataloging-in-Publication Data

Trottier, Maxine.
A safe place / written by Maxine Trottier; illustrated by Judith Friedman.
p.   cm.
Summary: To escape her father's abuse, Emily and her mother come to a shelter
where they find a safe place to stay with other women and children in similar
circumstances.
ISBN 0-8075-7212-8
[1. Women's shelters – Fiction. 2. Family violence – Fiction.]
I. Friedman, Judith, 1945- ill. II. Title.
PZ7.T7532Saj 1997
[E] – dc20   96-34555
CIP   AC

Art medium: graphite.
Text set in Goudy.
Design by Scott Piehl.

For Women's Community House – M. T.

Thank you to Neelie and Kelsey – J. F.

One morning when Emily woke up she was not in her own bed. She was not in her own room. She wasn't even in her own house. Then she remembered. She was with Mama in the big white house on the hill.

They had come to the house in the middle of the night a while ago. It had been one of the bad times, and Mama and Daddy had been arguing. Emily was afraid as she lay in the dark listening to them shout. She hoped Daddy wasn't hitting Mama again. Emily could hear Mama crying. Emily lay very still in the darkness and cried, too. She had tried to be good, but no matter how good she was the fighting didn't stop.

Later that night when the house was quiet, Mama
came to Emily's room.

"I've had enough. Hurry Emily," she whispered. "You
can only take Teddy." They rushed to the car and drove
down the dark streets. Emily thought about Daddy all
alone in their house. What would he do without them?

Mama stopped the car in front of a big white house. Then she and Emily got out. When Mama rang the bell, a woman opened the door. Mama was crying. Emily held Teddy very tightly.

"Hello," said the woman as she patted Mama's shoulder. "It's okay. You're safe here."

And it did seem safe. When Emily and Mama went to bed that night, it was quiet and warm. There was no one yelling and no one throwing things. Other moms and kids lay sleeping in the big room.

"When are we going to see Daddy?" Emily whispered.

"Not right away," answered Mama quietly. "We will be here for a while. You will see Daddy again, Emily, but we have to plan so many things first." Mama held Emily closely, and they fell asleep.

As the days went on, Emily saw many people in the
big white house on the hill. Everyone had something to
do. Jane answered the door, and all the moms took turns
cooking the food. There was a large, busy kitchen where
something always smelled wonderful. Sometimes Mama
helped in the kitchen. It made Emily feel good inside to
see Mama smile while she worked.

There were moms and kids everywhere. They shared every room in the house. People talked to each other and to Jane. It seemed that Jane was always holding someone's hand or patting someone on the back.

Emily played with the other children in the shady yard. It wasn't always easy to get along. Some kids wouldn't share toys, and some kids hit. When that happened, Jane would say, "We don't ever do that here. Here we talk it over."

Every day Emily went to the playroom and painted
pictures. Sometimes she painted herself, and sometimes
she painted Daddy or Mama.

"This is Mama when her arm broke. Daddy is saying
he's sorry that he hurt her," she told Jane, showing her
a painting. Jane hugged her. She said that the picture was
a very good one and that nothing bad would happen to
Mama's arms here.

One fall day when it was cool and bright, they all went outside and planted tulip bulbs in the damp soil around the house.

"When these come up in the spring, they will have flowers," said Jane. "They will make us think of the kids and their mothers who have come here and gone away to start a new life."

Emily dug a little hole and dropped in a bulb. She covered it with earth and patted it down. There it would sleep, safe and quiet in the ground until spring.

"Will we be here to see the flowers, Mama?" she asked.

"No," answered Mama. "We will be leaving soon to live in our new apartment, but we can come back to visit."

"I miss Daddy, Mama," said Emily softly.

"Well," said Mama, "let's see what we can do about that."

And so that night, Emily called Daddy, and they had a long talk. Emily felt better.

Finally one morning, they packed up their things and got ready to go. Mama had her purse and Emily had Teddy and they each had a little suitcase with some clothes from the big white house. Mama would be going back to work now. Emily would be going to a new school. Mama hugged everybody, and everybody hugged Emily.

Just as they were starting to leave, the doorbell rang. Jane looked out through the peephole, and then she opened the front door. A little boy and his mother walked in. The boy was holding his stuffed rabbit. He seemed so scared.

Emily remembered how she had felt on the night she came to the house. As Mama and Emily came to the door, Emily leaned over and whispered to the little boy, "It's okay. You're safe here."

Then she and Mama walked out into the sunshine.